JUMAH'S WORLD

A TALE FROM KALIJOR

PAUL LELL

My thanks to everyone who contributed to this work. To my wife for her art, editing, and support, and to Wolvris who, despite the tribulations of his own life, responded with not only a cover, but four interior images, answering my panicked call each and every time with a calm, "here you go." To Nami for her humbleness and willingness to be involved after the judging, and to Clarice for throwing in with the rest of us crazy people! And most of all to the reader of this book, for your contribution to the lives of children in need. I thank you all, and am humbled by your generosity.

To say that he hated the city of Talanor would be, at best, an understatement. However, he would never use the word 'hate' to describe his feelings about the city, rather he would describe it as an overall feeling of claustrophobia accompanied by a constant desire to dash back out into the freezing cold of the Southern Wastes. It wasn't through any need he might feel to use more complicated words, or because he was afraid some lover of the subterranean city would overhear him disparaging their home that he wouldn't use the word 'hate'. No, he would not use that word because that was a word he felt should be reserved for those things in life that were generally worse in nature than anything else one had ever encountered. It was not a word to be used, or taken, lightly and to his credit he had used it only once in his entire life; on that terrible day so long ago.

Craning his neck, he tried to locate the ceiling of the massive cavern the city was built within. The dim, constant illumination seemed wholly inadequate for the task, but his supernatural sight still allowed him to see the far off roof over head. Its smooth, stone surface long ago chiseled clean of any stalactites in an effort to prevent them spontaneously breaking loose and impaling some unsuspecting visitor to the city.

Finally, turning away from the stone orifice to get ready for his day, he shook his head slightly. Long, unrestrained blond hair shifted back and forth across his back. He just didn't understand how people could feel comfortable living so enclosed all of the time. He longed for the open air of the Plane of Serenity, cool grass beneath his bare feet and blue sky over head. This trip couldn't end soon enough for his taste. He didn't like the cold feeling of loneliness this place seemed to bring about in his normally happy demeanor. Jumah sighed heavily as he looked once more out the window into the dimly lit expanse beyond the room he had been forced to stay in the previous night.

Brushing the thoughts aside, he crossed the short distance to the tiny bed. There he had laid out his few things, and before he sank back into those unpleasant thoughts, set about preparing for his day. With smooth, practiced ease he slid the leather harness over his shoulders and fastened the belt snugly around his waist. Testing the harness for a tight fit he then picked up a small leather cord and used it to restrain his mane of hair behind his neck in a loose tail. Finally, he picked up his swords from the bed. Each one was just a bit over three feet in length, with the bottom foot being handle and gleaming, simple blades that ended in razor-sharp, chisel-like points. The weapons gleamed like mother of pearl, playing with the artificial light in the room like a gem might play with the light of day.

Holding the weapons firmly he spun them a couple of times, creating a blurred arc in front of him as they sliced through the air with a satisfying swishing noise. Gracefully, he worked his way through a sword kata, slashing the air with a series of quick movements to his left and right, planting his feet in firm stances with each movement. He completed the form, sliding the twin blades home in the crossed scabbards on his back, just as a barely audible, almost frantic knocking sounded off of the thick hardwood door to his room.

"And so it begins." He said aloud. He crossed to the ancient looking door and released the overly complicated locking mechanism. He watched in wonder as a series of gears, pistons, and levers whirred into motion on the door's surface. He guessed that it took a full thirty seconds for the mechanism to release its hold on the stone threshold surrounding the door, but the diminutive person he knew to be waiting outside obviously had some understanding of the process because as soon as the gears and machinations began to move, the knocking stopped.

As the door slowly opened, Jumah looked upon his tormentor. She was a tiny thing. Not that such needed to be said when speaking about a gnome, but even as gnomes went, she was a tiny thing. She looked up his six and a half foot frame and grinned from ear to ear, revealing a set of brilliantly white, perfectly formed and spaced teeth. Her tiny face was thin and pleasantly featured and her button nose was adorned with a set of tiny, round spectacles that were barely as big around as her clear, steel grey eyes. Her hair was, for lack of a better way to describe it, a complete disaster. If it had been properly cared for it may have been lovely but as it was the mop of fiery orange strands was pulled straight back from her face, restrained through some unknown means into what looked like a large explosion frozen forever in time on the back of her miniscule head. And to complete the picture, she was wearing what had surely, at one time been a very nice, expensive robe. Now however, it had been totally destroyed by the liberal application of grease and soot over an unknown, but presumably long, period of time. Any form of preparation he could have made for this assault on his senses would have been completely swept aside as soon as she began speaking.

'Good morning sleepy head!" She chirped, her grin growing impossibly wider.

Jumah put on his best 'Help me for god's sake I am locked in a cave with a cheerful gnome' smile and nodded down at the woman. She barely crested the top of his kneecap, even with her hair taken into account. "Good morning m'lady. How are you?"

She beamed up at him. "Spectacular. Couldn't have hoped for better weather for the expedition!"

Jumah looked over his shoulder toward the window in his room and tried to imagine any other type of weather Talanor could experience. Turning back to the gnome, he opened his mouth to ask the question but stopped short. He saw the twinkle in her eye that said she was more than willing to talk, at some great length no doubt, about the subtle variations that were likely to occur from day to day in the climate of a cavern such as this. Finally he settled on, "Good to hear. So what's the plan?"

She looked almost sad for an instant but bounced back quickly, grey eyes sparkling. "The porters are ready with the equipment and all of the permits are in order. All we have to do is make our way into the old mines and start looking for it. I anticipate no less than a ninety nine percent success rate on this expedition given current circumstances and forecasted trends in the geo-thermal activity in the area. Furthermore, if my calculations are correct there is also a high degree of likelihood that we will encounter at least three mechanized stationary sentry units within the immediate proximity of our final destination." She smiled again.

Jumah blinked at her a couple of times before nodding at her with a complete lack of understanding. "Sounds good. We should probably get moving then eh?"

When he was done here he was heading straight to the Plane of Serenity and running flat out until his body could simply not take it any more and forced him into unconsciousness. He had to have been completely out of his mind to think he could work with a gnome, in a cave, on an expedition. Yes, what was left of his people needed the money for supplies this winter, and then there was Riana, he wanted to get her something nice. But he was beginning to have second, and third thoughts about this.

Gimbobble, that was the gnome's name. She turned around in a haphazard way that made Jumah think of a toddler just learning to walk, and moved down the hall toward the main door of the small stone structure where he had spent the night. He wasn't sure if it was her house, or her workshop, or just some other strange machinery-laden building in the city, but he knew he was glad to be free of it the moment they stepped out the front door. He was no stranger to the emerging sciences of the world, and he was far from being against its development and proliferation, but something about Gnomish contraptions always set him on edge. Maybe it was their propensity to explode at the most inopportune moments. Maybe it was their inexplicable need to be so much more complicated than was ever really necessary. Either way, he could never feel comfortable around their gadgets.

The short walk to the mines Gimbobble spoke of seemed to take forever. He worked exceedingly hard to not step on her or leave her behind. Each of his steps was equivalent to a dozen of hers and while she was positively bubbling with excitement, she seemed totally unconcerned with how long it took to get there. Maybe it was all the time she spent reviewing supply lists and notes on how the expedition was supposed to proceed, all while trying to navigate the needlessly complex streets of Talanor.

Finally they arrived at the cave in question. There was a pair of frightened looking gnomes standing at the entrance to the mine, each of them bearing a pack on their back that was easily five times their weight. Between them, they had a stretcher-like platform laden with supplies and equipment positioned between them.

"Are we ready?" She chirped as she stopped in front of the pair. They both looked up at Jumah from his mid-thigh area with pleading looks on their faces, afraid to say anything. Finally the complete lack of response seemed to click in Gimbobble's brain as an affirmative and she moved off into the mine boldly. "Alright then here we go!"

The two porters sighed sadly, picked up the equipment between them and followed their diminutive leader into the darkness of the mine.

As they moved into the mine, his claustrophobia began to settle in on Jumah. He forced his apprehension into the back of his mind by focusing on the road ahead. The entire time they were moving through the dark cavern, lit by the half-dozen small glow-stones hanging from their equipment, Gimbobble was carrying on about how she expected to find the lost Dwarven capital city of Kal'ek T'nal that had been buried since the great war eons ago.

She went into extensive detail on the architecture and craftsmanship of the capital building. Rattling off minutia about the first royal family carving it from the stone, and subsequent generations adding to the original structure when it could no longer sustain their ever-increasing progeny. She spoke around food and drink about the tradition that grew into families adding their own wings to the structures when they took over the running of things.

She swore that by the time the city disappeared from the world, the capital building would have been easily the size of every other structure in the city combined. Then she started talking about the foundries, smithies (as if every person in Kalijor didn't already know that

Dwarves made all the best gear), and taverns (they also made by FAR the best ale).

Finally, Jumah had just stopped listening to her squeaky little voice as it droned on and on in animated fashion about Dwarven this and Dwarven that. Instead, he concentrated on the simple act of putting one foot in front of the other despite his claustrophobia's best efforts to make him turn around and head for the open skies. It took him a moment to realize that the drone of her voice had stopped. Looking over his shoulder to where the trio of gnomes stood stock-still he raised an eyebrow at them as they stared in his direction with looks of horror on their faces.

Briefly he felt a surge of panic run through his body. He quickly forced it back and looked forward again to try and makes sense of what was bugging the gnomes. Looking into the darkness, he realized that he must have had his head in a bucket not to hear what had brought them up short. Rolling down the tunnel like a tidal wave was the very distinct sound of mining equipment being used to scrape away chunks of rock and stone. The sound of wheels turning and boulders tumbling. Underlying it all was the sound of... "Singing?" he whispered to himself. Not just any singing either. No, this was singing in a foreign tongue with raspy, squeaky voices that could only be produced by one particular, ornery, fork-tongued creature. "Kobolds.." he finished to himself.

"M...m.....maybe we should t....t....turn b...back....." One of the porters barely managed through chattering teeth.

"N...no... we must..... press on....Right Master Wataru?" Gimbobble tried to sound stoic from behind the heavy equipment skiff the porters had been carrying. Her unkempt shock of grease-streaked hair and grey eyes all that was visible over the top of the equipment as she tried to peer over it.

Unseen by the group, a small, scaly creature crept toward them in the dark shadows of the mine. A wicked dagger was held at the ready eyes watched the group standing about deciding what to do with themselves. Adapted over time, its clawed feet made no sound on the rocky terrain as stalked ever closer. It was sure this would be the one, this would be the time that it could prove to its elders that it was ready, ready to hunt, ready to sire a family. All it needed to do was bring back

one of the little gnomes, bloody and broken, for them to see…
Positioning itself perfectly for the attack it crouched down low, rustled
its leathery wings and, gathering its strength, pounced.

"It's your coin. If you want to press on, then we press on."
Jumah said as he nonchalantly snatched the leaping Kobold out of the
air without looking. The diminutive creature howled and screamed,
flapping its tiny bat-like wings uselessly as it scratched at Jumah's arms
and stabbed his flesh repeatedly with its dagger. Jumah held the creature
closer to his face, just out of its weapon's reach and eyed it with his blue
eyes that seemed to glow in the darkness.

The Kobold, realizing that any wounds it actually inflicted on its
captor apparently instantly healed themselves, stopped stabbing and
scratching and looked him in the eyes. Its narrow, forked tongue darting
out to taste the air silently before disappearing back into its pointy face.

Suddenly Jumah was back on familiar ground and his
claustrophobia all but evaporated, momentarily forgotten while he dealt
with the creature. Glancing over at Gimbobble, he turned back to the
Kobold and spoke in a calm, even tone. "How would you like to do me
a favor?"

"Are you sure this is a good idea, Master Wataru?" Gimbobble's voice was near cracking as she spoke from behind Jumah's leg where she apparently felt safe and secure from the terrifying Kobold.

"Gimbobble, I asked you to call me Jumah." He smiled to himself as they followed the Kobold through the darkness of the ever deepening mine shaft. The claws on its feet gave it purchase on the rocky terrain, letting it move easily while Jumah and the gnomes struggled to keep pace. Jumah was sure the creature would have bolted by now, if it weren't for the thin rope he had tied about its waist.

"Oh." She said in a suddenly hurt voice. It seemed obvious that she was now very much outside her comfort zone and had no idea how to handle it at all. "But that creature… attacked us. Are you SURE we should trust it to lead us around its friends?"

"The only thing I am sure of right now Gimbobble, is that you are going to get caught under my foot if you keep trying to hide behind my leg like that." He paused for a moment, realizing that the gnome would probably be terribly offended at the vocalization of her terror, despite the fact that she obviously was. "Even for a scientist of your understanding, a Kobold is a pretty easy creature to motivate. You just have to understand what it is they are seeking, as with any creature really."

She separated herself slightly from him but made sure he stayed between herself and the Kobold. "And what is it that motivates a Kobold? Aside from bloodlust?"

"You see, that's the problem there. You assume it wants death and destruction."

"But Mas... er... Jumah... Every Kobold my people have ever encountered has attacked us. All evidence suggests they are bloodthirsty killers and where the evidence points, the logical mind must thereby follow."

"Ah ha!" Jumah proclaimed as he ducked under a low-hanging rock in the ceiling. "There's your problem! You assume that what makes logical sense to you should also make logical sense to others as well. A Kobold is a very different sort of creature from a gnome now isn't it? So why would its logic work out the same as yours?"

Gimbobble sounded disgusted as she replied, "Jumah, the very point of logic is that it works the same for everyone. THAT is why it is CALLED logic! Logic by definition must make sense to everyone in the same way for it to be called logic."

Jumah smiled, there was nothing better in the world than flustering a gnome. Except maybe a good long run through an open field. Damn he missed the open plains. Snapping himself back to the here and now he gave a light tug on the rope to make sure their Kobold friend knew he was still paying attention. "That's where you are wrong Gimbobble. You see, logic, like so many other things in life, is subject to the views and opinions of the individual. As an example, it makes logical sense to me for everyone to do fifty push-ups every morning before getting on with their days. That way everyone will be fit, healthy and strong."

She nearly fell over in the dim tunnel at the thought of doing push-ups, at all, in any quantity. "Mast... Jumah... That is preposterous. Most people are incapable physically of doing fifty push-ups. And

16

furthermore it doesn't make logical sense for everyone to do so when we need so many other things from people, like the honing of the intellect and scientific theory!"

"Oh I agree those are important things as well. Logically speaking however, if you take the time and develop the discipline to hone your body, then it follows naturally that you will develop your mind as well. Mind and body as one. It should happen no other way. Logically speaking."

"Well I'm sorry but that simply doesn't make any sense to me. It seems like much of the time used to develop the body could be diverted to developing the mind and greater strides could be made in that direction. I'm afraid that your logic is faulty in the matter."

"And yet it makes perfect sense to me. And have you ever wondered why the standard parts for a mechanical sword sharpener include a cog and three spinners when a cog and three sprockets would clearly add the benefit of more torque?"

The little gnome stopped in her tracks and stared at him, taken aback by his sudden insight into her world. "You present an interesting case Jumah. I shall have to consider it further."

They had been traveling quickly down hill for several hours before the steep decline began to level out again. Finally, the Kobold came to an abrupt stop and refused to go any further into the mine. Jumah leaned down and conversed intently with the creature in its native tongue while Gimbobble and the others watched. Finally he produced a small leather pouch from one of his larger belt pouches. Turning the pouch over in his hand, several small, brown objects fell into his open palm, each looking like a tiny wooden spiral. The Kobold's eyes went wide in amazement and its bat-like wings fluttered with uncontained excitement. As Jumah carefully poured the objects back into the pouch and drew the strings closed the Kobold actually began to dance from foot to foot with its arms stretched out in front of it.

Jumah removed the thin rope from the creatures waist, thanked it and bowed deeply before it, then handed it the small pouch. The Kobold snapped up the pouch and disappeared back up the cavern so quickly that it appeared to the gnomes as nothing more than a blur.

Gimbobble looked back at Jumah with her eyes wide in amazement. "What was in that pouch? What were those things?"

Jumah smiled at her knowingly. "Brume tree seeds."" He said simply as he looked up the mine shaft behind the vanishing Kobold.

"Brume tree seeds?! But that's absurd! Brume tree seeds are worthless!"

"Maybe to you they are worthless. But most Kobolds live their entire lives under ground. The majority of them will never lay eyes on a brume tree. As such, their seeds are highly prized among the Kobolds. So you see, it is a good thing to know your neighbors. When you know how to motivate someone properly you can get amazing results."

"So it would seem." Gimbobble said with an air of disbelief. "So, why did you turn him loose? We have not reached Kal'ek T'nal yet!"

"He refuses to go any further because of the ghosts. It doesn't really matter though, he got us past his friends and that is all we really needed him for."

Jumah looked down at the gnomes, when the tunnel seemed suddenly and strangely silent. What he saw was amazing to him. All three gnomes were looking at him with looks of pure disgust on their faces.

"What?"

"Master Wataru. A person of your apparent learnedness should know there is no such thing as ghosts!"

Jumah looked down at them all as they nodded their heads in unison, confirming the nonexistence of ghosts between them. Never mind the fact that Jumah had in the past encountered ghosts, indeed fought them with his magical blades. They were by no means a figment of the imagination and in fact, they were exceedingly difficult to destroy. However, he had no desire to get into a debate on the nonexistence of ghosts with three gnomes in the bottom of a mineshaft. Besides, he was fairly certain that the banging and clanking noises described to him by the Kobold had very little to do with disgruntled spirits.

He smiled at them. "Of course not. But as you say, they are simple creatures…" he was afraid his heavy sigh would betray his true feelings on the matter.

The gnomes seemed satisfied with his response and the group moved on into the darkness. Before long, they began to hear clanking and whirring noises echoing off the walls of the shaft. The faint sounds bounced and reverberated off of the rough walls, doubling back on themselves again and again, making it impossible to determine their source.

Cautiously they forged ahead into the growing din. Before long it began to sound as though they were in a Dwarven smithy, hammers pounding away at metal implements and the roar of bellows driving flames to impossible temperatures. The cacophony was nearly unbearable and prevented the gnomes from hearing Jumah's order to stop moving.

Instead they all piled into his still form, dropping their equipment in a heap on the ground and squealing in surprise as instantly the noise in the cavern stopped completely.

"Shhh…" Jumah hissed quietly while placing his foot on a small metal tool that was clattering away from the scene of the traffic accident.

After a moment, a soft whirring noise approached them and Jumah crouched down low. Keeping his legs under him he placed his right hand on the handle of one of his swords and his left behind him in a gesture to silence the gnomes.

The whirring sound grew louder and was eventually joined by a soft, rapid clicking.

"That sounds like metal scraping stone. Probably some kind of digging machine." Gimbobble whispered, causing Jumah to cover her face with the palm of his hand.

As he did so, a mechanical spider with long, spindly, metal legs spreading out from a central core, five on either side, rounded a bend in the mine shaft ahead of them. It would easily have come up to Jumah's waist except that the machine was moving along the top of the shaft, its long legs stretching to either side of the tunnel.

"Amazing!" Gimbobble exclaimed through Jumah's hand.

Instantly, the mechanical contraption swiveled its boxy metal head toward them. Glass, stalk-mounted eyes focused in on them with a series of whirring noises. It seemed to pause for a moment, going silent before pulling one of its legs from the wall. Raising it up, the point directed toward Gimbobble.

"Damnit!" Jumah cursed as he lurched to the side in time to intercept the deadly appendage as it sliced through the air toward the gnome. The metal limb speared his left shoulder pushing him back with the force of the blow and eliciting a low grunt.

With one fluid motion he drew the sword his right hand was gripping and brought it down on the mechanical leg. A loud metal clang ringed through the cavern and sparks fell in a bright arc. As the leg was wrenched from the thing's body, the free end fell toward the ground, dragging Jumah with it. He used his left hand to pull the appendage free of his shoulder and held it up between himself and the spider. Looking at the leg he saw a massive bend in the metal where his sword had struck it, but it was not severed by the magical blade.

"This does not bode well." He said as he tossed the thing to the ground and took a fighting stance.

The spider took a moment to twist its eye stalks around and examine the damage to its body. Then it wheeled around again, focusing on Jumah as a red light began to glow through its glass eyes.

Jumah slipped his second sword from its scabbard and moved them both into the path of the thing as it lunged bodily at him. Metal on metal reverberated up and down the mineshaft as Jumah intercepted the automaton's lunge. He stepped forward into an offensive stance, tossing the machine to the ground.

It rolled over with a clamor and wheeled around to face the group again. Buzzing and clicking as it moved with surprising speed, it lifted up another appendage and lanced it toward Jumah's chest.

Jumah twisted himself out of the way, deflecting the needle-sharp leg with one of his swords as he drove the other one forward, catching the machine off guard. The tip of his sword struck home, shattering one of its glass eyes to pieces and making it reel back away from him.

He switched to a defensive stance in front of the gnomes and waited for the machine to make its next move. He didn't have to wait long, as a pair of limbs shot out this time, the remaining eye glowing bright red in the darkness.

Jumah jumped up, coming down on top of the legs and pinning them to the ground under his bare feet. A flash of metal at the corner of his eye had him bringing up one of his swords in time to parry another leg but he wasn't fast enough to block the fourth as well. The metal spike drove through his chest with ease, piercing his lung and ripping up the muscles and bones. He grimaced in pain and staggered, releasing the automaton's legs.

Gimbobble shrieked as she watched the leg appear in the center of Jumah's back. There was no way he could have hidden it from them, the tip of its leg had probably been more than a foot exposed on his back. The device left its offending leg speared through Jumah's body for a moment, before finally pulling it free and backing away again. Forcing himself to his feet as the gnomes watched in amazement; he planted a strong kick on the inner joint of the leg, driving it free of his body and the wound on his back closed itself up before the gnomes' eyes. He was obviously much more than the human they had thought they were hiring.

"We need to put an end to this. If there are more of these things, this noise is sure to attract them." Gimbobble finally managed.

"Agreed." Jumah breathed heavily, his lung only just beginning to work again. "This ends, NOW!"

Lunging at the spider with his swords leading the way, he deftly changed direction mid-charge as the thing shot out a pair of legs to intercept him. In an instant he was on the wall, feet planted firmly as he bounced out of range of the spider's appendages. Before gravity had time to force him to the ground, Jumah had sprung across the shaft to the opposite wall, twisting around in mid-air to plant his feet solidly on that wall.

Again, a pair of legs whipped out and drove deep into the rock face where Jumah had been an instant before. The mechanical contraption seemed to hesitate briefly, apparently unsure of what to make of the situation. That was all the time Jumah needed. Twisting around in mid-air once more, he planted his feet firmly on the ceiling above the machine and drove himself down, sword points first.

His right sword drove cleanly through the contraption's head, his left through its blocky body, mid way between the legs on either side. Finally, he swung his legs down and stomped, bending the metal of its back into two perfect impressions of his feet and driving the thing bodily into the stone floor. The thing's internal mechanisms ground to a halt and slowly its one remaining eye went out.

Wrenching his swords out, Jumah inspected the metallic beast clinically. Tapping its head with his foot and kicking at its side to see if it reacted at all, he decided to make sure it was well and truly disabled. With a mighty stroke, he sliced half way through its thin metal neck. Raising an eyebrow curiously, he took another swipe and severed the neck completely.

"Interesting." Gimbobble said as she scuttled forward and began inspecting the thing. She was positively twittering with excitement.

"I'll say." Jumah commented. "These swords cut dragon hide with less trouble. That is no ordinary metal that thing is made of."

"Amazing! Simply amazing!" Gimbobble muttered to herself as she poked through the damaged hulk of the mechanical contraption. "Master Wataru, could you open up its chest cavity a bit more please? I need to get a closer look at its internal workings."

Jumah smiled slightly as he resheathed his swords and bent down to the machine. He placed his fingers inside the gash his sword had made and pried the metal armor open with a grunt of effort. The material was definitely much stronger than any armor he had encountered before in his travels. While his strength was enough to tear and bend the metal away from the gears and cogs of its internal workings, it was with a great deal of effort and the sharp metal bit painfully into his fingers.

Even before he had opened the gap significantly, Gimbobble was prodding at the cogs and gears of the machine excitedly. Jabbering like a school child and grinning from ear to ear, the fear only moments past was already long gone from her mind. "My goodness! Look at this! They have used a size sixteen oscillating cog here for the drive mechanism."

Standing up from the wreckage, Jumah pulled a clean cloth from one of his belt pouches and wiped the blood from his hands, inspecting them to make sure the wounds had closed. If they remained open, it would be a sign that the machine was either magically enchanted or bore a significant silver content. He sighed in relief as he inspected his perfectly healed hands.

He wasn't entirely sure if he should be happy or not however. On one side, this meant that these machines could do him little lasting damage, although his gnome charges would certainly be worse off. On the other side it meant that the contraption was capable of putting up a significant fight through the use of mundane materials. There could easily be more of them wandering around. In large numbers, they could amount to serious trouble for them.

With another sigh, he tucked the bloodied cloth back into his pouch. Turning to check up on the Gnomish porters, who were shakily moving their rack of equipment closer to where Gimbobble was now pulling small pieces out of the metal corpse.

After several hours of waiting for the three gnomes to finish their dissection, Jumah finally decided to set up camp for the night and busied himself with setting some blankets on the stone floor of the mine shaft and clearing a spot for a small fire over which he prepared a simple stew with some water and a few of the dried provisions they had brought along.

After much prodding he finally managed to get the trio to eat something. Before they had even set their half-empty dishes down, they were already diving back into their work. Even the two porters had forgotten their trepidation and showed a genuine interest in the project, cataloging the contents, configuration, and potential purpose of the machine's inner workings.

Jumah eventually moved closer to the gnomes and looked over their shoulders at the myriad of pieces and parts. All of the parts were neatly organized into piles that seemed to make little sense as Jumah examined the scene, looking for some rhyme or reason.

One small pile contained several gears, or cogs, he wasn't sure which, some small coiled springs, a few bolts, and one of the creature's spindly legs that they had disconnected at the body joint.

Other piles bore similarly strange combinations of things and each time he saw them pull something new from the wreckage, one of them would place it delicately in a specific pile.

Leaning in over the trio, he sighed heavily. Waiting a moment for them to ask him what was the matter, he finally cleared his throat and spoke in a normal conversational tone, when none of them reacted. "You know. We should be moving on in the morning. It would probably be a good idea if you three got some sleep."

"We can't sleep. We're in the middle of a comprehensive post mortem investigation into this machine's internal functionality." Gimbobble replied without taking her eyes off the gaping hole in its body.

"Be that as it may. I must insist that you all get some rest. Even if it is just one at a time for a few hours."

"Nonsense. We gnomes can go days without sleep when we are working on a project such as this!" she said proudly, looking up at him with a glint in her eye. Jumah wasn't sure if it was from the light of the lanterns they had brought, or some internal insanity specific to the Gnomish race that caused the glint, but he wasn't ready, or willing to discuss the matter with her.

"Look. I am your guide and protector on this expedition and as such I must insist that you get at least SOME rest. If you are unwilling to get some rest then as soon as you are done with your investigation of this machine I will escort you back to Talanor and you can find yourself another guide."

The look on Gimbobble's face changed immediately from one of mischievous mirth to abject horror. "Oh! Oh no! That simply won't do! You are the only person that answered my call. No one else wants to accompany us on this expedition!"

"Then I suggest that you heed my advice in the matter and take turns getting a few hours of sleep before we head out. I have no desire to keep you from your work, but we must all be able to act when the time comes and exhaustion is not a state that is conducive to that end."

Eight hours later, each of the gnomes had reluctantly laid down for a few hours. Jumah was certain that Gimbobble had not slept a wink even though her eyes had been closed. Her hands were continually moving in the air above her as if she were manipulating and examining pieces of the mechanical spider. When she 'awoke' she immediately set about criticizing everything done while she was away from the project. She cast several icy glares in Jumah's direction as he set about cleaning up the camp and getting them ready to travel again. He simply shrugged at her and kept on with his business.

Finally, the small gnome proclaimed that they had done enough research for now and the group could move on. She was certain however, that there was more to be learned from the dismantled contraption and insisted that they plan to stop upon their return toward Talanor. She had pulled out a strange silver box with a few faintly glowing crystals on its surface. Numerous gears and cogs affixed to the sides were spinning continuously despite the box being disconnected from the spider's body.

"What is that?" Jumah asked skeptically as she strapped the strange device to the platform suspended between the porters.

"I believe it to be the source of the automaton's power. It seems to be drawing energy from these crystals using light refraction across a wide spectrum prismatic spray that focuses specific wavelengths of light on a precariously balanced actuator that oscillates, thereby transferring the light energy into kinetic energy that drives a progressively increasing cascade of gears eventually resulting in the transference of said energy from this component into the body of whatever mechanical contraption it is imbedded."

Jumah stared at the gnome for a moment before clearing his throat. "So it's a box that changes light into mechanical motion."

Gimbobble glared at him with a ferocity that only the incredibly short are capable of mustering before saying, "I just told you that!"

Jumah smiled at her before replying, "Then what should really be eating at you is where they are getting their light from down here in these mines. Moving forward to lead the way deeper into the darkness of the mines, he left her there to ponder a moment before scrambling to catch up.

With the lanterns at his back, Jumah's natural ability to see in the blackness was limited by their harsh glow. The ever-increasing mechanical noises emanating from ahead of them created a wash of cascading noises around them that turned into a dull roar, muting the effectiveness of his keen hearing.

"We surely must be drawing near our destination by now." Gimbobble's voice barely squeaked over the din.

"Either that or there is some sort of gnomish trade show going on down here." Jumah replied through gritted teeth as the sound threatened to overwhelm him. The disadvantage of heightened senses, he thought to himself, was that they were easily offended by overly powerful experiences.

"Why would gnomes have a trade show down here in these mines?" Gimbobble asked seriously.

Jumah's shoulders sagged slightly as he sighed, silently admitting defeat. gnomes simply had no capacity for sarcasm. All he knew was that if he didn't get out of this noise soon, his ears would start bleeding. That's when it happened.

They rounded a corner and stepped into a huge, cavernous space. It stretched out well beyond the range of Jumah's vision, but the change in the constant din of mechanical clicking and clanging told him that it was a cavern easily the size of the one in which the entire city of Talanor was built.

"What is this?" Gimbobble breathed, barely audible, "It must be Kal'ek T'nal!"

"Don't get ahead of yourself Gimbobble. Douse the lights."

"But, Master Wataru, we won't be able to see…" She began to protest.

Jumah wheeled around on the gnomes and stuck one finger in each of the lanterns, squelching the tiny flames. "It isn't us being able to see that I am concerned about. It's them being able to see us."

As the lights went out, the mechanical noises filling the chamber stopped as well, eliciting a collective gasp from the gnomes.

"Stay put." Jumah hissed as he slipped off into the cavern, leaving the gnomes standing alone in the darkness.

As they shuffled their feet and tried to see in the darkness, the sound of mechanical legs striking stone began filling their ears. Their nervousness was palpable as they imagined an army of the mechanical spiders bearing down on them in the darkness.

"M….master Wataru…" Gimbobble's voice broke as she whispered to the darkness, hoping that she was not truly left alone there.

The sounds of the machines grew louder and louder, accompanied now by the crumbling and rolling of small stones as chunks of the stone firmament were dislodged.

As the sounds increased in volume, becoming nearly unbearable to their tiny ears, a panic began to set in on them. Their vivid imaginations, fueled by Gnomish mental acuity, drew detailed images of them being dissected and their parts being categorized by an army of mechanical spiders. They began to shift uneasily, bumping into each other and the equipment. They were near the limits of their courage. Ready to scream for Jumah or run wildly into the darkness, when a loud metallic clang echoed through the cavern, accompanied by a brilliant flash of blue-white light.

Stunned by the sudden flash, Gimbobble wasn't sure but she thought that she had seen Jumah silhouetted in the glow. His twin swords skewered through the central mass of a mechanical spider, Jumah had almost certainly been perched lightly on top of it. An instant later the light was gone and the gnomes were left with a brilliant white spot in their vision and questions about what they had just seen.

The mechanical scuttling sounds shifted direction, their timbre changing as the automatons seemed to readjust their course to deal with the more threatening of the intruders. Another brilliant flash of light revealed Jumah once more, now on the far side of the group of attacking spiders. Landing soundly on the back of one, he drove a sword into its body. As it crumpled to the ground, Gimbobble gasped.

"He's attacking their power supplies!" She muttered with a combination of respect and disgust in her voice. She was very happy that they might not actually end up on the spider's menu. The fact that he had quickly learned how to destroy them and obviously had no reservations about doing so, caused her a pang of regret at the loss of the mechanical contraptions.

A cacophony of mechanical noise left the gnomes' ears ringing as the spiders tried to coordinate their efforts at attacking their quarry. Flashes of light began to erupt around the cavern. Each location seemed impossibly far from the last. Jumah would be attacking one of the machines, and then instantly be on the other side of the group attacking again.

The gnomes stared in awe, watching the flashes criss-cross the space. They had no idea how quickly he was actually moving as many of the flashes began to blend together, lighting a small portion of the cavern.

Finally, the noise and light came to a sudden end. In the deafening silence the gnomes began to shift on their feet again. The brilliant white splotch in their vision faded, leaving them to wonder what was happening in the all-consuming darkness of the giant cavern.

Suddenly, one of the lanterns flared to life again. The three gnomes jumped. Turning to face the light, the gnomes were greeted by the form of Jumah.

He was standing there, almost casually, leaning against the gnomes sled full of equipment, weapons neatly stored in their scabbards on his back. He was covered nearly from head to toe in blood, but not a single wound could be seen on his body.

"Master Wataru!" Gimbobble gushed. "Are you alright?! That was… the most amazing, frightening, despicable…"

Jumah quirked an eyebrow at her as he retrieved a water skin and a small cloth from the gnome's equipment. Slowly he began wiping the blood from his face and body, stopping her tirade with a wave of his hand. The gnomes quickly relit the remaining lanterns and gasped at the veritable sea of parts on the cavern floor. Eagerly they began poking about in the wreckage of the mechanical army that lay at their feet.

After a few moments of examining various parts and pieces, Gimbobble walked up to him tentatively. Feeling very unsure of herself, she opened her mouth several times as if to speak before anything escaped. "Master Wataru I…"

Jumah looked at her for a moment, realizing how serious she looked. "Yes?"

"I…er…" She looked as though she was having trouble finding a comfortable way to stand as she seemed to struggle internally with what she was about to say.

"Yes?" Jumah prompted her.

"I noticed that you… That is… I… I mean, you're all covered in blood!" She finally managed, as if it explained everything she was thinking and trying to get out.

"You know Gimbobble… Sometimes, I think your most impressive feature is your iron-clad grasp of the obvious." He smirked as she balked at his statement.

"But you haven't any wounds! That's the point Master Wataru. You are covered in blood, and you haven't any wounds on you!"

"You know… I noticed that."

"And the one you fought earlier. I saw it stab you, straight through! Just there!" She pointed at the location where the first mechanical spider had skewered him.

Jumah sighed heavily as he crouched down to look her in the eyes. "Are you sure you saw what you think you saw?"

She eyed him clinically for a moment before nodding her head slowly, purposefully. "I did."

"Then what is your conclusion?" He asked, eyebrow raised again, as if challenging her to a duel of intellects.

She knitted her tiny eyebrows together, turning around and pacing a small path in front of him. With one hand crooked under her chin and the other at the elbow of the first, she began to think out loud. "You bleed so you must not be undead. *But* you don't actually show any signs of having actually been damaged, so you must either heal extremely quickly or you are somehow displacing the damage."

"Truly, you have a dizzying intellect." Jumah grinned at her.

"Wait 'till I get going!" She beamed.

"So you are not undead, but you could be a polymorphed dragon." She turned sharply as if to punctuate that possibility. "Although they would be much tougher to damage and as you said, and I myself confirmed, that the automatons were made of merely mundane metals, it is unlikely that they would be capable of damaging a dragon thusly. Therefore, I can clearly rule out your being a dragon." Turning on her heel, she dismissed the line of thought with a quick nod.

Jumah shook his head, a smile spreading across his lips as he watched Gimbobble reason things out.

"But there are so few creatures that can heal that quickly and still function in society, *and* are active during daylight hours. Most of those tend to be deities and gods, but if you were a deity or a god then you would probably not be bleeding at all so I can clearly assume you are neither of those."

Jumah kept on wiping himself with the cloth while she continued her pacing and verbal reasoning. Ticking off each possibility with that decisive turn, she offered only a few more options before planting her feet and turning towards Jumah.

"Given what I know of the species of Kalijor, and what I have seen of you first hand, I can make only one logical assumption. You are a lycanthrope." She looked at him triumphantly before resuming her pacing. "Judging by your speed and agility, I think I can safely assume that you are not one of the larger felines. Therefore the only logical conclusion is that you are a werecheetah."

Jumah continued wiping at the drying blood, not looking at her, or acknowledging her statement in any way.

"What I don't understand is why you would risk your life by being in a city and dealing with so many people when lycanthropes are a declared kill-on-sight species. Everyone knows that lycanthropes can not adjust to civilization and are a dangerous race to anyone not of their own kind."

Jumah looked very serious all of a sudden. He had stopped wiping at the blood and raised his head to watch as she paced and talked, more to herself than to him, or anyone else in the area. "So, what does logic dictate?"

She looked at him briefly, thrown off track for a moment, but quickly fell back into her groove. "Logic dictates that if you are taking such a risk, then you are either insane and wish to die, or…" She looked up at Jumah with a strange look on her face.

"Or…" Jumah looked back at her, his own expression somewhere between hard and almost afraid.

"…or," She continued, "the stories about lycanthropes are much exaggerated."

Jumah simply waited for her to finish, immobile and silent.

"Obviously you are a well-adjusted, competent individual with marketable skills and certain social graces. You most certainly have a reasonable grasp of logical thinking, even if you are wrong quite a lot…" She eyed him for a moment. "It simply must follow that not all lycanthropes are as evil as we have been led to believe from the stories."

Jumah relaxed visibly.

"My only question then is this, how much of the stories are false, and how much is truth?" She looked at him pointedly.

"I apologize for deceiving you. It's not something I enjoy doing… What questions can I answer for you?"

"You have nothing to apologize for Master Wataru. If I were hunted because of some distant cousins of mine, I would most likely not open conversations with full disclosure either. Let's begin with, is it true that lycanthropy spreads through the transfer of bodily fluids?"

Jumah sat down, facing Gimbobble. "It is true only of the wolves. We feline lycanthropes can only pass it on to our offspring."

"I see. And the feral personalities?" She began looking around for some sort of writing instrument with which to make notes.

"The wolves again." Jumah said softly. "We have been at war with them for centuries. Unfortunately, the way they reproduce makes them a difficult adversary to overcome. Once, we were close to beating them for good. That was when they rampaged through the streets of several small villages, turning everyone they saw."

"The beginning of The Blood War." Gimbobble nodded excitedly, forgetting Jumah's lycanthropy. "That was when the rest of the races of Kalijor declared war on the lycanthropes and destroyed any that were found, no matter where they were or what they were doing. Thousands were killed in just a few weeks time!"

"Yes. Much of my family among them. Since that day, all lycanthropes have taken precautions to keep themselves unknown. You are one of a select few that know my secret Gimbobble. Can I trust you with this?" He asked her in earnest, no malice or threat in his voice, it was a simple question.

She looked at him seriously, searching his deep, blue eyes. Finally, she smiled a genuine smile, her normal energy much more focused and sincere. "Of course you can Master Wataru. You have more than proven yourself to us."

Jumah inclined his head to her. "Thank you Gimbobble. There is just one more thing though…" He spoke as he stood up, crumpling up the blood-soaked cloth in his hand as he turned away from her and took a few steps toward the pile of destroyed mechanical spiders. The other two gnomes were busily looking for salvageable components, oblivious to the exchange.

"Yes?" She looked almost worried about what he was going to say.

"Please, call me Jumah." He said over his shoulder as he waded off into the wreckage.

She smiled at him and set about poking through the mechanical contraptions.

As it turned out, the vast cavern they had found themselves entering was merely an antechamber to the actual city proper. Here they found half a dozen large buildings that were most likely used as inns, taverns, and merchant facilities back in the days when there had been a fully functioning city here. At one point, Kalek'Tinal had been the capital of the Dwarven empire and as such it had played host to a steady stream of adventurers, travelers, and dignitaries from other cities in the realm.

The trappings of civilization were evident, although centuries old. There were still wooden and stone goblets, bowls and fixtures littered throughout the buildings. Most of the items were still sitting out on surfaces as if they had been recently used and were waiting for the people to return from a town meeting.

The only thing stranger than the state of those artifacts was the complete absence of any kind of metal. Not just swords, knives, and armor. Every single piece of metal had been taken from the place (as if they had been collected with extreme intent). No silverware, no pots or pans, no jewelry of any kind, items held together with metal bands or rivets had long since collapsed.

"It is more than likely used in the creation of other mechanical automatons." Gimbobble remarked matter-of-factly as the small group poked carefully through the great room of what must have once have been a respectable inn.

"So, is this what you needed to see down here?" Jumah asked, almost hopefully of the little gnome.

"As telling as this actually is, it is not really what I was after, no."

The two porters were on the other side of the room, poking through a pile of furs, looking for anything of value as Jumah and Gimbobble spoke to one another in hushed tones. There was more than a little concern in Jumah's voice as he spoke. "Look, Gimbobble, I need you to know that as strong and fast as I can be, these machines, whatever they are, seem to be incredibly resilient to damage. Even from my enchanted blades."

Gimbobble looked up at him with a quizzical expression on her face. "But Ma…. Jumah…" she corrected herself hastily, "You seem to have fared extremely well against the automatons thus far."

Jumah sighed heavily, "I know, but we had a distinct tactical advantage here. One, they didn't know we were coming, and two, the combination of my speed in the sudden darkness. We made out all right but that isn't a series of events that we should be relying on to work in our favor going forward. Circumstances can change quickly and I don't want your lives on the line if that happens to our disadvantage."

Gimbobble seemed to look more thoughtful than usual for a moment before raising an eyebrow in Jumah's direction. "What if we could turn another factor in our favor?"

Jumah crossed his arms across his chest and eyed the gnome suspiciously. "What factor?"

Gimbobble grinned from ear to ear as she turned and made her way back out of the inn. She motioned for him to follow as her little legs carried her toward the entrance of the cave where the graveyard of parts lay strewn about.

Jumah followed her with a look of deep concern lining his face. He wasn't at all sure he liked the situation, especially given a gnome's propensity for overly complex plans. "Gimbobble, what are we…"

"Reinforcements!" She cut him off suddenly as she spun around in the middle of the junk pile to face him, arms spread wide to indicate the pile of scrap at their feet.

Jumah gaped at her. "You can't be serious…" He finally managed to get out.

"Why not?" She mused. "They were obviously built by someone, and as such they have been given a set of instructions. Replicate, protect, scavenge, and so forth. Who is to say that we cannot rebuild those instructions to suit our own purposes?"

"You mean beside the fact that we have only the barest idea of how the things work in the first place?" Jumah replied as patiently as he could under the circumstances. He thought he may have come off a bit testily.

Gimbobble hadn't noticed, or was just too excited to care. Either way, she kept plugging onward with her line of thought. Bending to examine one of the destroyed machines more closely.

She spoke to herself as much as to Jumah. "All we need to do is discern where the machine's control center is and derive what sort of mechanism is in place to provide it direction." She pulled a rolled up leather skin from one of her pockets and opened it on a clear patch of floor with a flick of her wrist, revealing a long row of tidily organized tools, each in its own little loop, pocket, pouch, or enclosure. After a moment's consideration she deftly whipped a couple of tools from their places and began fiddling with the head of one of the mechanical spiders.

"I would imagine that it is nothing more than a difference engine, using some sort of preset, recorded documentation to provide checksums to balance environmental factors against. Probably using the Stombublean fractal algorithm to account for differences in perceptions… If we can just decode the checksum template then we will have an easy road into the machine's reasoning faculties…"

Jumah stared at her as she plunged further and further into her own world. He opened his mouth to say something, but was cut off by an ear-piercing shriek from the inn. In the space of a heartbeat, Jumah turned and was out of sight, but not before blurting out authoritatively, "Stay here. Don't move from this spot. I'll be right back."

He burst through the inn's doorway, swords drawn. Pausing in the center of the large room to get a handle on the situation. In the corner, behind the pile of furs he spied a stone staircase, heading up to the higher levels of the massive inn. A trail of wooden bowls and goblets leading up the stairs was a good indication as to where the gnomes had gone. Jumah vaulted across the room and took the stairs six at stride.

On the next level, he saw a long hallway with a series of crumbled doors on either side. He estimated twenty in all as he searched the rooms behind them for any sign of the gnomes. Another shriek sent him dashing down the hall toward its source. At the end of the hall, the corridor made a right hand turn, presenting him with another long hallway. With as many doorways decorating its walls he began to think he wouldn't find them in time. But this time he caught sight of a doorway at the end of the hallway with the pile of desiccated wood in its threshold obviously disturbed The faint patter of tiny feet on wooden floors confirmed that the gnomes were near-by.

Vaulting over the wooden debris in the doorway he quickly took in the situation, scanning for any signs of trouble.

"What is it?" Jumah bellowed as he spied the two gnomes cowering in the corner, behind the disintegrating remains of the bed's mattress in the corner.

One of the gnomes raised a shaky hand and pointed toward the corner of the room near the remains of the door. Jumah spun around and adopted a defensive stance, swords at the ready as he crept toward the spot indicated by the gnome.

Jumah narrowed his eyes, focusing all of his senses on the corner. A large wooden wardrobe and a small end table with a stone basin on it stood silently. He saw no signs of a mechanical fiend anywhere. Prepared for anything, he lowered himself in an effort to see better under the wardrobe without compromising his defenses. As he was about to get a clear line of sight beneath the wardrobe, he heard a small scurrying sound from within the furniture. With a questioning look over his shoulder toward the cowering gnomes, he slowly sheathed one of his swords and reached out to the handle on the wardrobe's door.

With a yank, he jerked the doors open and took a step back, holding his sword at the ready and braced for an attack. But no attack came. The wardrobe was empty, save for a pile of shredded, disintegrating, musty old cloth at the bottom. Again, he looked over his shoulder at the gnomes, who were trying as hard as they could to sink into the floor of the room, shaking like leaves in the autumn wind, eyes glued to the pile of fabric.

Jumah returned his attention to the pile and, with the tip of his sword began sifting through it. Suddenly, a large rat darted from beneath the pile, hit the floor with a small thump and skittered out the door and around the corner with such speed that Jumah thought it could possibly give him a run for his money. This event, coupled with the loudest, highest pitched scream he could ever remember hearing in his entire life, caused Jumah to spin violently around. His magical blade cleanly bifurcating the ancient wooden wardrobe caused it to fall to the ground in a heap. A piece of the decimated wardrobe crashed into one of the legs of the end table next to it, causing that wood to splinter. The end table tilted violently, dislodging the heavy stone basin on its surface. The basin, teetering for a moment, slid off and rather than thumping solidly on the floor, or even rolling around the room a bit, crashed through the rotted floor boards, causing a ripple of seismic activity to wash around the room.

The sound of the wood cracking and splintering all around him caused his keen ears to hurt and the hole made by the basin quickly enlarged to encompass half the room. As he watched the almost comical chain-reaction the portion of the floor upon which Jumah stood collapsed. He dropped through the void beneath his feet and with a sudden impact and an even louder crash, his world turned to darkness.

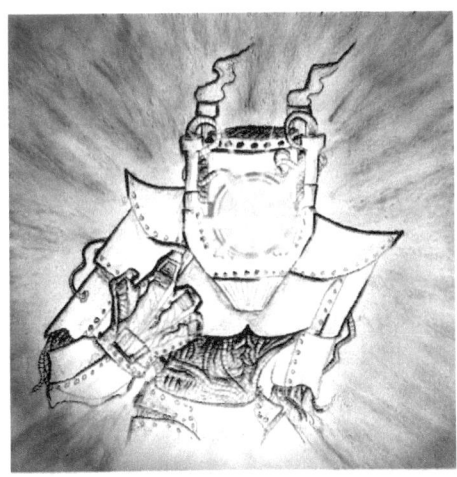

Jumah came to with a groan, opening his eyes to total darkness. A few attempts at movement told him that he was buried under the debris from the floor, which was likely why he was shrouded in darkness.

"gnomes." He sighed quietly as he steeled himself. With a gentle but constant force he began to push with his arms in the direction of least resistance, slowly working to extricate himself from the wreckage. Dust and debris began to shower down around him in little rivulets as he applied his strength to the task. A sudden change in the sound around him caused him to pause.

Listening intently, he heard nothing save for the expected cascades of dust and debris coming to a rest around him. After several long moments, he was ready to dismiss it as his imagination and resume digging his way out. Then he heard a new noise. A metallic clicking sound mixed in with some scraping and scuffling noises sounded as if it was nearly on top of him.

"Nothing is ever easy when gnomes are involved." He grumbled under his breath. Pushing against the debris with all his strength, he steeled himself for more trouble. Falling chunks of smashed flooring and walls, obscured his view and what little remained was clouded with kicked-up dirt and rotted wood dust. Getting his feet under him and throwing his arms out over his head, he freed himself of the last of the debris and stood up. In the faint light, he tried to get a clear view of where he was.

A heavy metallic thud to his right told him that there was indeed a mechanical contraption near by and with a quick twist, he was facing the over-turned spider with one of his blades in hand. The mechanical spider, overturned by his final thrust to escape, squirmed and writhed on the ground in an attempt to find purchase with its ten wickedly sharp appendages. Not wasting any time, and certainly not the opportunity, Jumah leapt from the debris pile and landed bodily on the spider, driving the point of his sword into the central mass where he knew its 'heart' to be.

His blade pushed through the armored metal skin of the creature and a shuttering whine escaped its hollow interior as in response, internal workings seized up and the thing died a grinding, metal-on-metal death. As the spider rattled out its death, Jumah heard a faint, hollow moaning sound from somewhere off to his right. Quickly he extricated his sword from the creature's belly and slid its twin out of the scabbard across his back.

With a quick look up to make sure there was no danger above him, he realized that he had fallen not only through the floor of the second level of the inn, but also the main floor, and possibly the cellar floor as well. Moved off in the direction of the noise, he padded silently across the remarkably clean stone floor.

As he advanced into the darkness it became clear that he was, at least in part, still in the inn's basement, although the structure had been extensively modified from its original design. Any stone walls that once existed had been all but removed, leaving only the natural stone of the cavern. Cut smooth and polished to a mirror shine, the floor sloped downward at a mild angle.

Jumah's head swam. His claustrophobia tried to drive him back out of the tunnel screaming as he moved down the corridor, surrounded by pristine, immaculately carved and maintained granite. He simply couldn't fathom anyone going to this much trouble over a simple corridor. To make matters worse, he was hearing more and more mechanical noises coming from down the tunnel. The only thing that kept him moving forward was a sense that these noises were somehow different than the rest.

There was something different down this tunnel and he had to know what it was, to the point that his desire to know was able to keep his need to panic in the tight space in check. The sound grew louder with each step forward and after a few minutes the faint glow of some sort of artificial light source bounced off the mirrored stone surfaces of the tunnel.

As he approached, the deep mechanical moaning sound changed into the sound of some massive thing taking deep, rasping breaths. Somehow, the sound was still very…mechanical. Fighting against the trapped feeling and panic rising up in the pit of his stomach, Jumah squeezed the handles of his swords more tightly in his hands and concentrated on placing one foot in front of the other.

The sound grew ever louder and the eerie light continued to get brighter and brighter. The light was a constant, unflickering, greenish glow that seemed to be moving in time with the raspy, mechanical breathing.

Slowly the tunnel began to widen and the downward slope steepened, transitioning into a set of immaculately carved stairs. Taking the stairs one at a time, Jumah's breathing began to slow and he relaxed a little bit as the tunnel seemed to be turning into a much larger chamber. The green light remained ahead of him, bobbing slowly up and down to the breathing sound, although the light itself—shining directly at him as it was—made it impossible for him to make out the shape of whatever was supporting the strange light.

All at once, there was a flurry of mechanical clicks and whirrs. In an instant Jumah was surrounded by more of the mechanical spiders. They were on all sides of him faster than even he could have seen, dropping from the ceiling of the cavern and scuttling down from the walls to close off his escape route. However, unlike their brothers in the caverns, these spiders did not immediately attack him. Rather, these automatons seemed to be waiting for something, fore-legs poised to strike should the order come.

Spinning around slowly, it took him only a moment to realize how much trouble he was in. In this enclosed space, with dozens of the things surrounding him and poised to strike, he was in deep. He might be able to do some serious damage before they got him and he wasn't even sure if they could actually kill him, given his lycanthropic blood. He did know that they could cause him a great deal of pain and bury him under a mountain of metal, preventing him from getting away or ever seeing the light of day again. Suddenly, he felt a pang of longing for the open air tear through him with a heartless lack of concern for his current position.

"Who...are...you..." A mechanical voice ground out, hammering through his momentary reverie.

Snapping his eyes toward the origin of the sound, he saw only the strangely bobbing light. Squinting against the green glow, he tried to make out the form behind it. Based upon where the light was suspended he could tell only that it was probably some twenty feet tall. Anything more than that was obscured by the green light overwhelming his vision.

"My name is Jumah Wataru." He replied tentatively, eyes shifting back and forth to the mechanical army that surrounded him.

"Why...are...you..." The voice sounded like a pipe organ in a bad state of disrepair.

"Why am I what?" His eyes flashed between the light and the army of spiders, sure that the wrong answer or comment from him would cause them to flood in upon him without warning. They remained menacingly still, as only a mechanical foe could.

"Why...are...you..." The voice repeated.

"Why am I here?" Jumah prompted.

"Affirmative..." The voice thundered.

"I am here to protect my companions. They are explorers, here to discover the fate of Kal'ek T'nal." He flexed his grip on his swords as he spoke, keeping an eye on the army of spiders.

There was a long pause then, accompanied by several long, loud moans and clicks, much like a gnomish water boiler straining under the stress of too much pressure and about to burst. Finally the voice returned once more, "What... is...Kal'ek T'nal..."

Jumah grimaced, surely Gimbobble or one of the other gnomes would be better suited to this sort of interaction. Although—he smiled to himself as the thought occurred to him—they may be more likely to incite a war from these things with their gnomish logic. Finally he looked back toward the light and replied, "This city is Kal'ek T'nal."

Another long, groaning pause. "What...is...city..."

The realization broke over Jumah like a wave at high tide. This thing was just learning how to communicate... "Look, this is shaping up to be something of a longer conversation than I would like to have while under the constant threat of attack. Would you mind calling off your spiders so we can talk a little more comfortably for a while?"

This time the groaning and clicking went on for several long minutes as the thing seemed to be considering what he had said. Finally it came back with, "You...will...not...attack..."

It didn't sound much like a question to him, but Jumah wasn't sure this thing really knew the difference. Still, he decided that the first gesture should be his if this thing was really trying to understand him. Moving very slowly so as to not startle his friends he stood up straight and very carefully raised his swords above his shoulders and slid them home into their scabbards across his back. Once the blades were settled in place he held his hands at his sides, fingers open and palms facing the green light.

"As long as you do not attack me, I will not attack you."

All at once a veritable symphony of mechanical clicking and scraping surrounded him. He flinched at the sudden eruption of noise, but quickly realized that the mechanical spiders surrounding him were disappearing into the deep shadows of the cavern. Within moments, they were all gone from sight with the exception of a line of sentries blocking the top of the stone stairs Jumah had descended into the cavern. Obviously this was a conversation he was going to have to see though to its conclusion.

"Thank you." He offered with a bow in the direction of the light. "Now as to your question. A city is a place where people, such as myself, live and do business together."

"People...like...you..." The voice droned.

"Yes. I am a person. One of a great many different types."

"No people here..." The voice was slightly less choppy, and the tone was changing, as if someone was tuning the pipe organ while they were playing it.

"No. Not for a very long time now. However, this used to be Kal'ek T'nal, the city of the dwarves. We have come to see what remains of the city."

"You are dwarf..." The voice told him.

"No. I am...something else..." He tried to put it as delicately as possible without inciting any sort of trouble.

"Others are dwarf..." The machine offered in response.

"Others?"

"Three others. Smaller than something else..."

Jumah almost laughed out loud. Clearly he was dealing with a blank slate here, although it was obviously capable of learning very quickly. Already it was sounding more like a living person when it spoke. "My companions are gnomes." He offered back.

"gnomes and something else. Other people?" This time it finished off sounding as if it had actually asked a question.

Jumah was suddenly having doubts. He could imagine the conversation moving very quickly into areas of knowledge that he simply didn't know anything about, and what would happen when he didn't have an answer for this thing? It was very intelligent, but what would be its response to frustration? Could it even get frustrated? Was it capable of feeling any emotions at all?

"There are many races on Kalijor. The gnomes. lycanthropes like myself," he was loathe to admit openly to most people that he was a lycanthrope, but he suspected that in this case full disclosure may be the best course of action. "There are also humans, dwarves, elves, ogres, trolls, goblins, and many more species. The dwarves used to live in this city, many centuries ago."

Again, a long pause filled with mechanical breathing, groaning and clicking. Finally, "What is your purpose here?"

Jumah was amazed at how quickly this mechanical thing was learning to express itself. He was also more than just a little bit concerned about what was going to happen when it had learned everything it could from him, or if he gave it an answer that it didn't like. "As I said, the gnomes are here as explorers, to learn what became of Kal'ek T'nal. We mean no harm to you."

"You have attacked and destroyed my appendages." The statement was matter-of-fact, not accusatory or even angry sounding, simply a statement of being.

Jumah flinched again at the statement. He hoped they had not irreparably damaged the situation. "I am sorry about that. The spiders...your appendages, attacked us. I accept full responsibility for those attacks. I am the gnomes' protector on their expedition and it was I who did the damage."

More churning and clicking sounds punctuated the silence that followed. Jumah waited in tension, ready to spring into action at the drop of a pin if the situation turned against him.

"You are not like the others." The voice finally replied.

"Others? What others?" He raised an eyebrow curiously.

"They are smaller than you. Smaller than your gnomes. They scrape away at the walls and take many crystalline matrices."

Jumah's mind clicked into overdrive, what could it be... then it suddenly slammed home. "Kobolds!" He nearly shouted out.

"Kobolds." The voice repeated. "What are kobolds?"

Jumah tried to think of a way to define a Kobold. Most would make it sound like some sort of annoying little rodent. Very few people shared his desire to understand the motivations of creatures. "The creatures that live in the upper caves, above Kal'ek T'nal. They have a compulsion to collect things that are shiny or that attract their attention. They don't mean to be bothersome but they are sometimes a little difficult to get along with."

"They take the Crystaline Matrices that I need to extend my reach."

"Crystaline matrices... Gems? Like the ones inside your... appendages?"

"Affirmative. The matrices make up the core of my processes and energy supply. Without the matrices I am unable to create new appendages."

"I am sure that something could be worked out with the Kobolds if you need the gems, there are many other things here in Kal'ek T'nal that they would find of interest and probably be willing to trade for the stones." He wasn't sure how amenable the Kobold nation would be to trade negotiations, but he thought they could be dealt with if they were approached properly.

"They do not talk as you do. They scurry into shadows and attack my appendages from concealment."

"I am sure they can be reasoned with, if you approach them in the correct way. In order to deal with a creature, you need only understand what motivates it to do what it does. If you open talks with them, tell them what you have to offer in exchange for the stones, then they may be open to negotiations."

"They run at the sight of my appendages. There is no opportunity to dialogue."

Jumah folded his arms across his chest and closed his eyes for a moment. Finally, he looked inquiringly at the green light hovering in the darkness. "Why do you make your appendages in this shape?" He pointed to one of the mechanical spiders.

Another pause punctuated the conversation. "It is the most efficient form." Was what followed.

"But you can make an appendage in any form you wish?"

"Affirmative."

"So create an appendage in the form of a kobold. Mimic their appearance so that you are less frightening when you approach them. This way you will be able to open dialogue with them."

Whirring, clanking, and great moans resembling an over-pressurized water boiler followed as the machine thought about his statement. After several very long minutes it finally responded, "What you suggest is complicated. My appendages are simple extensions of my body. Creating such an appendage, able to vocalize, will require me to fragment myself and relocate a portion of my being within the appendage."

"That does not sound pleasant." Jumah offered with a frown.

"It is what it is. If such a thing will aid me with the Kobolds, then such a thing will come to pass."

"I wish you nothing but success in your efforts to deal with the Kobolds. Would you mind if I asked you a couple of questions?"

"Ask your questions."

"How did you come into being?"

"I have memory of... a gnome... there is a workshop deep under the city you call Kal'ek T'nal where this gnome assembled my difference engine and set me to the task of solving complex mechanical problems. The results of those mechanical calculations eventually led to the creation of my motivational systems and power supply. Two-hundred eighty-seven point six cycles ago the gnome went out and never returned. I have since continued the tasks appointed to me before that time."

"So you were created by a gnome who went out and never returned. How long is a cycle?"

"One cycle is made up of three-hundred sixty-five intervals. One interval is made up of twenty-four rotations." The machine correctly inferred Jumah's next question.

"That sounds very similar to our method of time keeping. If that is really the case, then you have been down here all by yourself for nearly three-hundred years. What were your final tasks?"

"I have been tasked with procuring raw materials for the workshop."

"So you have been gathering raw materials for nearly three-hundred years now?"

"Affirmative."

"How large is this workshop? Where are you storing all of these materials?" Jumah couldn't help but be curious now that he had the machine talking.

"I have had to expand the workshop storage facilities numerous times."

Jumah thought for a few moments, rubbing the bottom of his chin with his knuckles. Finally he looked up at the light. "Can you tell me what a difference engine is?"

"Affirmative." The voice responded instantly.

Jumah waited a full minute before he realized that the machine was not going to tell him without some additional prompting. "Would you please tell me?"

"A difference engine is machine that is designed to weigh statistical probabilities and determine most probable outcomes after accounting for all possible variables."

"So you are designed to make decisions based upon known facts?"

"Affirmative."

"So let me ask you something. What information do you have concerning the disappearance of the gnome that created you?"

More clicking and whirring preceded the machine's response. "The gnome exited the workshop and has not yet returned."

"And given that the average life-span of a gnome is around five-hundred years or cycles, what is the probability that the gnome is still alive today?"

"Forty-three percent." The voice replied without a moment's hesitation.

"Good." Jumah replied. "Now, account for the fact that most gnomes do not move out on their own within the first fifty years of their lives and the fact that most do not begin working in their own workshops until they are around one-hundred years old. What is the likelihood now that your gnome is still alive and well?"

"Twenty-two point four eight percent."

"Excellent. Now, given this new information what do you make of your current situation?"

The machine churned and whirred for nearly five minutes before responding this time. Finally it came back with, "I calculate a less than ten percent likelihood of the gnome's return based upon new information."

"So, does this change anything for you?" He asked cautiously.

"It alters the statistical probability that the gnome will return and issue me new instructions."

"And if the gnome never returns. What will you do?"

"I will continue to follow the last instructions given to me."

"So you will continue to carve raw materials out of the mines for all eternity?"

"That would seem a likely outcome."

"Are you allowed to alter your instructions based upon perceived information?"

"I am not allowed to alter my base-level instructions independently, merely the way in which they are carried out."

"So you can alter how you follow the instructions but not the instructions themselves…" Jumah began to pace back and forth a little as he thought about what to do. On the one hand, this machine was down here harvesting raw materials and not bothering anyone else in the world, except perhaps the occasional scared Kobold. On the other hand, he had to consider the fact that this machine could be of use to the people of the world, especially to the smiths of Talanor who could likely make good use of three-hundred years worth of collected raw materials. Due to the state of the mines, it was no longer safe for people to come in after materials and they had begun to import their materials from much more distant sources. Working out a deal with this machine could provide a major boon to the economies of a great many cities in Kalijor. If he could find out to what extent the machine's creator retained control perhaps he could discover a way to make the machine work with the world. "Is the gnome that created you the only person allowed to give you instructions?"

"Negative. I am authorized to accept input from any individual able to provide the initiation phrase."

"And are you able to provide any hints as to what the initiation phrase might be?"

"Negative."

"I figured as much." Jumah replied.

As he set about thinking of what sort of password a gnome might use to control its mechanical creation, which could be just about anything, he was suddenly startled by a massive mechanical roar. "Deceiver!"

He looked toward the mysterious green light in time to see a gargantuan mechanical head lunge out of the darkness at him. It was a huge box-like affair studded with pipes, wires, and metal plates held on by some sort of metal bolts or studs. Its large green eye shone brightly in the center of its head and just above it was a tiny mark that Jumah could only just barely make out. Two snakes twined around one another in a circle, each one swallowing the other's tail. The emblem struck a chord in his mind. For some reason he felt that he had seen something like that before, although he couldn't remember where, or why it would have been important.

As the head loomed out of the darkness it was followed by a large metal body bearing thick arms, covered in gears and levers that moved and ground as the machine lunged forward. Its hands ended in three thick fingers and supported the bulk of the machine as it loomed over Jumah menacingly and his peripheral vision told him that the mechanical spiders were moving in around him again making their threatening clicking noises.

"What happened?!" He shouted back as he restrained himself from drawing his swords again.

"You keep me talking and distracted while your gnome friends prepare to move against me!" The voice boomed as the head moved within inches of Jumah's own face.

"I assure you I have no idea what they are up to. Please let me go talk to them. I am sure we can get them to understand what you are." He held his hands out from his body, keeping them clear of his swords as he implored the machine to listen to reason. "What are the odds that I stumbled on your lair with the express purpose of distracting you while my friends, who are ill equipped to defend themselves from simple Kobolds, try to attack you? Think about it! Weigh the odds. Do what you are supposed to do!"

The machine turned its massive head to the side for a brief moment before leaning back in toward Jumah and bellowing loudly, "Make them stop! Or I will!"

He didn't wait for the machine to do anything more. The sentry automatons gone from their post at the top of the stairs, Jumah was gone from the chamber in a flash. It took mere seconds for him to make it back to where he had crashed through the floor of the inn. With one leap, he was out of the hole and on the floor of the great room. Turning his head, he focused his hearing until he located the gnome's voices. Finding them, he was off like a crossbow bolt in the direction of their panicked ululations.

As he moved toward the gnomes, he realized they had been very busy in his absence. The two porters had made it back to the debris field where he had destroyed the last batch of mechanical spiders. Together with Gimbobble, they had managed to construct some sort of fortified structure from which they were launching grapfruit-sized chunks of the destroyed spiders at an army of advancing—and much better conditioned—spiders.

The gnomes were hollering to one another for more ammunition, to reload, tension a spring, pull a lever, or a myriad of other things as they continued to assault the advancing tide. Much to their credit, whatever they had constructed behind their make-shift wall seemed to be packing enough punch to knock the advancing spiders off their feet. Although as Jumah passed them, it appeared that most of the mechanical creatures were simply turned over and working to right themselves. Very few of the automations seemed to have suffered any real damage at all.

With lightning speed, he vaulted delicately off one of the spiders, leaping high into the air and dropping silently into the center of the gnomes' fortification. Facing the panicked inventors' backs as they loaded more of their damaged spider parts into the catapult they had cobbled together, Jumah stood up, unnoticed.

"Quickly get me another one of those heavy pieces. They seem to be having the best effect..." One of the porters yelled as he peered out a small slit in their wall at the surging sea of spiders.

"I'm having trouble finding them. We should have piled these by weight instead of size." His friend replied in a stress-high tone.

"Or perhaps you shouldn't have attacked them to begin with?" Jumah interjected. His simple statement nearly scared the gnomes right out of their skins. Gimbobble was the first to turn and look at him from her position at the firing mechanism of the catapult. Her startled look quickly changed to an excited smile as she took in the sight of him.

The other two seemed to have a much more difficult time processing his presence, trading confused looks back and forth between one another. It was Gimbobble who finally broke the silence following his arrival.

"Master Wataru, they told me you had been killed," was her simple opening.

Jumah raised an eyebrow at the two scared-looking porters before turning back to Gimbobble, "Yes, well the rumors of my demise would appear to have been greatly exaggerated. At any rate, what is most important at the moment is that you stop attacking the spiders."

The look of horror on the gnomes' faces deepened and they began shaking their heads violently. "But...but...but...They'll over run us in a matter of moments!" One of them stammered.

"It's just a matter of time before that happens anyway, you aren't doing any real damage to them. Besides, I have it on good authority that they won't harm us." He looked directly at Gimbobble as he spoke.

She eyed him very suspiciously, clearly at war with herself as to what should be done. Finally, the logical part of her brain seemed to win out over the emotions and she nodded. "Stop attacking them," she said simply.

Her companions shook their heads in violent opposition but a quick round of shouting from Gimbobble turned them around. Within moments they had backed away from the catapult and the piles of scrap metal they had been flinging at the army. Gimbobble slowly reached out to the back wall of their improvised fortification and lifted the bar that was holding the door shut. The metal-on-metal groan was nearly lost against the background of the swarming mass of the arachnid army bearing down upon them.

Jumah quickly stepped out and turned to face the onrush of mechanics and the three gnomes came up behind him, peeking out from behind his legs at the swarm.

"They've stopped." Jumah shouted at the army. "Now go back to your gathering."

The horde was less than twenty feet from the group and showed no signs of slowing down. Nor did they make any attempts at communication that the quartet could see. When the rush was within a half-dozen feet, Jumah spun around and nearly threw the gnomes into the fortification, slamming the door closed behind them. He turned to face the spiders with swords in hand.

"Don't make me do this. I thought we had worked this…" He was cut off by the sharp pang of metal being driven through his legs, arms, and chest. His body was driven to the ground under the mass of metal doom as they swarmed in on top of him. Jumah felt every attack tearing through him. Their weight crushed down on him like a landslide, knocking his swords to the stone floor and forcing the air from his lungs with startling efficiency. It was only through a monumental push of willpower that he flung his arms and legs outward from his body, dislodging the metal creatures by the dozens and flinging them away from him.

Forcing his legs beneath him, he snatched his swords up and rolled backward, away from the regrouping automatons. By the time he regained his feet, most of the open wounds on his body had closed up and his strength was returning. As if they sensed his resurgence of energy, the spiders rolled in on him again, but this time they were met by the keen edges of his weapons.

The cavern quickly devolved into a wash of noise, sparks, flying metal and screeching gears. Fighting in the light of the gnomes' lamps made the battle more difficult for him, but he knew there was no real danger of them killing him. It was the gnomes he had to defend and the best way to do that was to keep the spiders' attention focused on him.

As the attacking swarm's numbers thinned out, the attack began to slow. Jumah dared to think, for an instant, that the machine had finally called off his 'appendages' but the thought almost doomed him. No sooner had the silver thread of hope formed itself in his mind than there was a loud rumbling sound issuing from somewhere in the cavern. The floor shook. Chunks of rock crumbled from the walls and smoothed stone fell from the ceiling far above them.

Before he could locate the source of the seismic activity, the sound of shattering stone brought his attention around to the inn. As he looked on, the building shattered into rubble. Pieces of shrapnel gouged out huge furrows in the surrounding buildings and a cloud of dust billowed up from the remains of the building's foundation.

Through the thick cloud, he could hear the sounds of groaning metal and saw the bright, piercing, green light rising up from the ground. It swiveled around searching, until it was pointing directly at him.

Without a second thought, Jumah covered the span between himself and the machine. He looked on in amazement as the thing pulled itself up out of the cellar. Unfurling six impossibly long, insect-like legs, it lifted itself up some twenty feet into the air and raised its two arms up high. Its two massive hands spread their four fingers wide as if it were trying to shake off a grogginess brought on by over sleeping.

With a sinking heart, Jumah realized that the machine's hands and the tips of its spindly, needle-sharp legs were gleaming silver in color rather than the dull, flat, metallic color of the spiders. His observation did not go unnoticed.

"The master's books taught me all that I needed to know about you, Lycanthrope. When my appendages were unable to kill you in the tunnels I thought it best to divine the nature of your being before attempting to destroy you. But now your weakness is known and you too shall be added to my stores for when the master returns."

"And I had such high hopes…" Jumah said aloud as he dove to the side in order to avoid a lightning-fast stab from one of the machine's legs.

"To hope is a waste of energy." The machine bellowed as it lunged at Jumah with another of its spindly legs.

Jumah dodged the stab only to be snagged up by the ankle as the machine's hand plowed through the air.

Jumah screamed out in pain as the silver encircled his limb and squeezed in on his flesh. It burned as if he had plunged it into a pool of acid. The creature held it there, smoke visibly pouring out around the metal hand as it seared into his flesh like a brand.

Fighting the pain, he threw his weight forward and swung his swords around in a wide arc. Slicing into the machine's hand at the knuckle. He grimaced as sparks sprayed out from the point of impact. The blow rang true and the thumb fell away, dropping Jumah to the ground in a heap.

Then it hit him like a bolt out of blue clear sky. He had been helping Riana research some ancient books she had recovered while searching for one of the keys. One of the passages he had read was a reference to words and concepts that meant the same thing when looked at from either direction. Perfect circles within themselves, with no beginning and no ending.

He rolled up to his feet, quickly removing his weight from the damaged right ankle, still smoking lightly from the angry, blistered band encircling it.

"You can't play this game for long. You're going to run out of appendages." He tried to make his voice sound steady through the pain coursing up and down his leg and spine.

"Appendages are irrelevant. You will fall, just like the rest." The machine's pipe-organ voice groaned out.

"You may be right. But I know something you don't know." Jumah retorted as he tumbled out of the way of another of the machine's attacks. The leg buried itself two full feet into the ground near Jumah's head. As the machine brought itself around for another attack, Jumah surprised it by reaching out and grabbing the retreating leg-tip.

Clenching his teeth against the pain of the silver in his grasp, Jumah let the leg lift him into the air. Carefully judging the level of the machine's body he swung his legs up and around the top of the leg. Planting his feet on the narrow metal appendage, he dismissed the burning ankle and hand. Breaking into a full run down the leg, he wobbled slightly but his natural agility won out.

"And what would that be Lycanthrope?" The machine bellowed as it scanned the ground beneath itself for its quarry, unable to feel his movements like a flesh-and-blood creature could.

Jumah quickly pulled himself up the machine's torso and perched on its shoulder in a crouching position. When the machine's huge head swiveled around to face him its bright, green eye was mere inches from Jumah's face, the twin snakes on its forehead glowing eerily in the darkness of the cavern.

"Palindrome." Jumah said forcefully.

In a flash of brilliant light, the machine's brilliant green eye winked out and the hulking body crumbled to the floor with a deafening clamor.

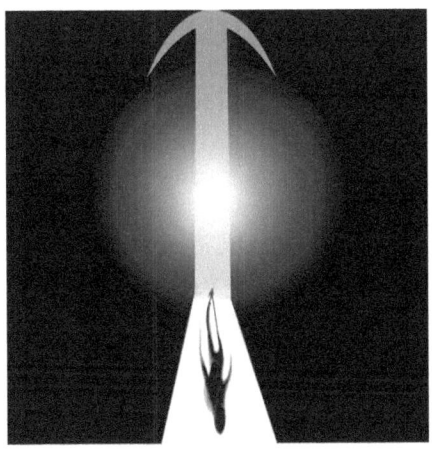

It was nearly two weeks and more than a few bottles of ill-tasting concoctions recovered from an alchemist's shop near by, before Jumah's wounds were healed enough for him to travel again. The group set up camp in that very alchemy shop and the gnomes had busied themselves with investigating the mechanical spiders and their master while Jumah rested. The bottoms of Jumah's feet had been charred by their contact with the silver plated machine and the thick blisters and burns around his right ankle had turned into an angry red and pink band that would surely become an ugly scar before long, owing to the fact that the machine had been applying significant pressure to the limb. He looked down at it wistfully as he pulled on his leathers, sitting on the edge of the bed. Their time in Kal'ek T'nal was done and they would be leaving for Talanor in a few hours time.

Exploration of the city and the areas beneath it revealed just how busy the machines had been over the years. Huge chambers, stacked floor to ceiling with smelted, formed, blocked, and refined materials. The sheer volume of materials the machines had extracted from the mines had surprised even the gnomes. Beyond those cavernous rooms they made a discovery that was horrific to say the least. Hundreds of clear cylinders filled with some sort of viscous greenish liquid held people of all kinds. Adventurers captured by the spiders and bottled up for some unknown reason, some with gaping wounds and others obviously alive when they were 'stored' in this grotesque collection. Jumah shivered at the thought of being trapped forever in one of those jars, remembering the machine's indication that he would be added to the stores.

Gimbobble created and read off new lists of instructions to the great mechanical monster which had become much more agreeable since the speaking of the code-word. The instructions made certain that the machine would not attack any more living creatures and Gimbobble had limited how many 'appendages' it would produce. In theory, there would be no more danger of the machine continuing its other work.

Unfortunately, the use of the code word to shut down and reprogram the machine also seemed to have erased any memory of what it had been doing previously. At least, that was the continuously repeated statement when they inquired as to the purpose of the hundreds of well preserved adventurers in its basement. Jumah remained skeptical as to the whole situation, but Gimbobble was positively bubbling over with excitement and after spending more than a week pouring over the notes of the gnome that had created the machine, she had devised a new set of instructions that, she said, could never be misinterpreted or put to the use of anything other than the benefit of all of Kalijor.

Arrangements had been made and the machine would begin exporting its collected resources up to Talanor using newly developed, specialized 'appendages'. Some of the spider-like automatons would also be accompanying the shipments up in order to reduce the likelihood of problems arising with the kobolds along the way. In short order, Talanor would be flooded with more readily usable materials than had been seen in years and the machine would keep them coming up out of the mines regularly.

Finally packed and assured that the machines could and would guide Gimbobble back to the city in order to continue her exploration and research, the small party hefted their bags. The pallet, originally carried by the two porters, rested on one of the new transport automatons. With a word, the party moved out of the cavern and into the tunnels.

The trip out of the mine was faster than the trip down. Led by the machines, laden with the first delivery of supplies, they were soon exiting the narrow mine shafts into the much more cavernous space where the industrial city of Talanor was built. Jumah's feeling of concern lifted only slightly in the larger space as he collected his payment, along with a substantial bonus from Gimbobble for a mission well done.

As he made his way toward the gates that would lead him back into the open skies of the frigid Southern Wastes, Jumah looked across the space to the entrance to the mines with a deep sigh. The sigh caught in his throat as he saw what he swore looked like a bright green light shining in his direction, but the light was there for only an instant and winked out so quickly that he wasn't even sure if it had really been there or if it was all just a bad memory that would stay with him for a long time to come.